SPY

LET SLEEPING DOGS SPY

MEET THE MEMBERS OF THE
SPY Society

ELISE WALLACE
Theater savvy Elise is the cast's go-to problem solver backstage.

PEYTON MITCHELL
As assistant director, Peyton has her eagle eyes trained to pick up clues.

LILY VESPER
Star of the show Lily works her actress magic on potential suspects.

CHARLIE LOPEZ
Dog trainer extraordinaire Charlie is talented at tailing suspicious persons.

BOWZER
Toto look-alike and honorary member of the Spy Society.

SPY Society

LET SLEEPING DOGS SPY

by Jane B. Mason and Sarah Hines Stephens

Illustrated by Craig Phillips

SCHOLASTIC INC.

New York Toronto London Auckland
Sydney Mexico City New Delhi Hong Kong

For the real girl Charlie—
reader and inspiring thespian.
—S.H.S.

ISBN 978-0-545-37470-5

12 11 10 9 8 7 6 5 4 3 2   12 13 14 15 16 17/0

Printed in the U.S.A.   40
First printing, February 2012

Designed by Jennifer Rinaldi

Chapter 1

"HOW'S THIS?" Elise Wallace asked, holding up a wicker basket with a piece of red gingham tucked inside.

"Perfect, as usual," Lily Vesper, one of her best friends, replied. The two girls were in the prop shop of the theater at their school, Proctor Middle. Another best friend, Peyton Mitchell, was with them . . . in body, at least. Her head was completely buried in a script for the play she was assistant directing.

"Dorothy enters right . . ." she mumbled, making a note in red ink.

"And goes directly to center stage!" Lily cried, throwing her arms wide. "Because Proctor Middle School finally built a theater that's worthy of my talents!" The three girls burst into laughter.

Lily was playing Dorothy in the state-of-the-art theater's inaugural production—*The Wizard of Oz*. And, like the rest of the cast and crew, she was over-the-rainbow enthusiastic about it.

"It's so exciting," Elise agreed. "Our first show!" She was about to secure the gingham to the basket when she saw Peyton's expression shift. The girl who loved to be in charge looked decidedly nervous. "Peyton, it's going to be amazing," Elise said reassuringly. "You've totally got this."

Peyton began to pace back and forth. "I know, I know," she agreed. "I just . . ."

Lily put an arm around her friend's shoulder. "You don't have to do it alone," she said. "There's an entire cast and crew behind you."

Just then Charlie Lopez strode through the door carrying an old-fashioned-looking suitcase under one arm and a small terrier under the other. "Special delivery," she announced, setting both down on the table with a flourish.

Peyton raised an eyebrow. "And you say you have no flair for the dramatic." Her dark eyes were alight with amusement.

Lily scratched Charlie's dog, Bowzer, behind the ears. "Hello, Toto," she greeted.

Peyton lifted her chin toward the case. "What's this?"

Charlie shrugged her shoulders as Bowzer climbed into the gingham-lined basket, sniffing intently. "No idea. I just found it by the main doors and figured it had to belong to the theater department."

Elise tilted her head and scowled slightly at the antique-looking luggage. She had spent the last week organizing all the theater props, and definitely hadn't come across this. "I've never seen it before."

"It's well made—that's for sure." Peyton ran her finger across the top of the case and peered at the letters stitched into the leather. "What do you suppose the Ss are for?"

"Who cares?" Lily stepped forward, rubbing her hands together as if she'd just found a buried treasure. "Let's open it and see what's inside!" She tried the latches, but nothing happened. The suitcase was locked. "Thwarted!" she cried. She leaned toward Charlie. "Where was it, exactly?" she questioned.

"Just inside the main doors. I practically tripped on it."

"Just sitting there?" Lily inquired, raising a brow. The girl was on the case.

"Yup," Charlie confirmed.

Peyton began to pace for the second time in five minutes.

"Um, can we deal with this later?" Charlie asked a little impatiently. "I was hoping to head down to the vending machines before you guys start rehearsal."

"And leave the mystery suitcase unopened?" Lily clutched her chest in mock horror. "I must know what's inside!"

"Um, Lil, it's locked, and it's not ours," Peyton pointed out. "We can't just rip the thing open."

"Why not?" Lily pouted. "Besides, there might be ID inside."

Elise turned to the workbench and pulled open a drawer. She had a remedy for situations like this. . . .

"We won't have to tear it apart," she announced a moment later. She held up a long, thin, wiry object.

Lily's blue eyes glimmered. "Ooooh, a lock picker!" she squealed.

Chapter 2

JUST MY luck, Charlie thought as her friends clustered around the suitcase. They were clearly determined to get it open.

"This is *your* fault," she whispered to Bowzer. After all, she'd found the suitcase when she was waiting for her mom to drop him off for play practice. Sure, Charlie suspected that Peyton wanted to "cast" Bowzer as Toto just so she would have something to do with the play—even if it was dog wrangling! But having Bowzer onstage was appealing in its own right, and he really did look just like Toto.

But while she was killing time outside waiting for

her dog chauffeur (aka Mom) to arrive, Charlie noticed a fancy silver car by the curb. It was a tiny two-seater—not the usual minivan. Charlie had been thinking that the car totally stuck out, when her mom honked. Since dogs weren't technically allowed on campus, Charlie'd tried to tuck Bowzer in her jacket while she hurried inside. She hadn't been watching where she was going when she'd nearly tripped over the suitcase by the main doors. The suitcase looked like it belonged to the theater, and Charlie didn't want to leave it there for someone else to trip on. With Bowzer still wriggling, she'd snatched up the suitcase and dragged it right along with her. Now, as she watched Elise try to pick the lock, she wished she'd left the thing where she found it.

Folding her arms across her chest, Charlie sat down on a stool with a giant sigh. Unlike her friends, she was not, repeat *not*, a theater person. And though she would never deny her best friends the things they loved, sometimes it felt like the theater was a fifth best friend that the other three shared, and she didn't.

The case was probably full of props and costumes

and stuff . . . nothing she'd get excited about. All Charlie could think about was food, anyway. She'd come straight to play practice from basketball and was starving!

Even with her fancy tool, Elise was not having any success cracking the case. She'd been trying to get it open for a five full minutes. Charlie's stomach growled. French fries danced in her head.

"How was basketball?" Peyton asked, as if she could tell her friend needed a distraction.

"Good," Charlie replied. "But Teresa Gordon was driving everyone crazy in the locker room. She kept complaining about having to wait until until next semester to play her first violin solo in the new theater. It's like she thinks she's the only one talented enough to christen the new stage!"

"Maybe she's just excited about our new state-of-the-art sound system," Elise suggested, fussing with the lock. "We all are."

Charlie shook her head. "No. You guys are excited. She's just full of herself. If I have to hear another word about her private violin lessons with the best violinist in the Tri-State Area, I'll barf!"

Bowzer barked his agreement while Peyton leaned in to get a better look at the lock. It was an unusual combination lock, Charlie noticed. There were only two rotating discs, and they had letters instead of numbers.

Elise was trying to pick the lock from a slit in the side, but it wasn't working. "I give up!" she cried, pushing the suitcase away in frustration.

Peyton traced the logo on the case with her finger. It was a single repeated letter: S. Leaning across the table, she turned both dials to S to match the design.

POP! The latches sprang open.

"You're a genius!" Lily cried, throwing her arms around Peyton. "An absolute, complete, amazing genius!"

Charlie patted Peyton on the back. "Good job, Madame Director. Now can we go eat?" She had the feeling it was pointless to ask, but couldn't ignore her growling stomach.

"No way. We have to see what's inside," Peyton said. "I mean, it could be anything!"

All four girls stopped for a second, considering the

contents. "Maybe it's filled with money," Lily whispered.

"Or fireworks," Peyton added.

"Ooooh." Lily made a mock-scared face.

Despite herself, Charlie was now genuinely curious. As Elise reached over to lift the top, she held her breath.

"Ready?" Elise asked calmly.

All four girls nodded. Elise lifted the top, exposing the contents.

Charlie groaned and sat back in frustration. It was just as she'd originally suspected . . . a bunch of dumb theater stuff.

Chapter 3

LILY LET out her breath as slowly as she could. Reaching into the suitcase, her hands trembled slightly. This was like a real-life treasure hunt!

"Look at this!" she cried, picking up a soft fabric case. She unzipped it and found a vintage jewelry set inside—a silver-and-rhinestone necklace and matching earrings.

"Nice," Charlie said, nodding.

"Nice? They're gorgeous!" Lily corrected, her blue eyes glimmering.

"Why don't you put them on?" Elise suggested. She paused in her suitcase exploration to latch the necklace around Lily's neck. Lily rushed over to the prop room mirror and admired her added sparkle. "How do I look?" she asked.

"Perfect," Peyton replied. "But maybe a little fancy for Dorothy." Elise helped her with the earrings, which were miraculously clip-on (Lily's mom was a holdout and wouldn't let her get pierced ears until she was thirteen).

Properly bejeweled, Lily glided back to the suitcase and pulled out a sleek pink and aluminum flashlight with the words "Flash Magic" stamped on the bottom. "What the heck is this?" she asked, rotating it in her hand.

"A very cool antique flashlight, that's what," Peyton replied, picking it up. She examined the bulb and the on-off switch. It looked old-fashioned, and yet . . .

Charlie leaned in close. "My grandfather used to collect old flashlights."

"Well, that thing is definitely old," Lily said, looking up from the suitcase.

"And still in perfect shape . . ." Charlie flipped the

switch, and the bulb behind the glass lit up, momentarily blinding Peyton.

"Hey," Peyton protested, shielding her eyes.

"Sorry!" Charlie quickly flipped the switch again and a red beam shot toward the ceiling. "Whoops!" She tried again and the light went off. She looked at Peyton sheepishly. "Third time's a charm?" she asked.

Peyton laughed and took the Flash Magic. "Maybe I should hang on to this—might come in handy as a backup spotlight."

Charlie jutted out her bottom lip in a pretend pout. "Are you saying I'm incapable of operating it?"

Peyton shook her head. "Of course not. I'm saying I could use this thing."

"Look at these." Elise held up a pair of cat-eye glasses with rhinestones in the corners. She slipped them on. "Stylish?" she asked.

Lily clapped her hands together. "Fabulous! I love those on you. But are they prescription? Can you see?"

Elise nodded. "I can see just fine—the lenses are plain glass."

"Check it out—the rhinestone pattern matches the jewelry," Peyton said, looking from Lily to Elise and back again.

"Supercool," Lily said, turning back to the suitcase. She could see that it was almost empty, and felt a twinge of sadness. The treasure pillaging would soon be over.

"What else have you got in there?" Charlie asked. Lily ran her fingers over the satin lining and pulled out something in another soft case. "Any guesses?"

"A sewing kit?" Elise wondered aloud.

"A snack?" Charlie asked hopefully.

Lily paused for dramatic effect, then opened the little pouch and let its contents slide onto the table. It was a silver pocket watch, with flowers and vines engraved on the back.

Before anyone could say anything, Charlie swooped in. "Cool. Something else that's useful!"

"Are you calling my jewels useless?" Lily huffed.

Charlie smirked. "Of course not. Highly useful for brilliant actresses. But since Peyton got the flashlight I'm glad to see something else that's more . . . utilitarian."

"Nice backpedal," Lily said with a grin. "But my earrings are waaay better than your pocket watch."

Peyton gave Lily a serious look. "They're not yours. None of this stuff is ours."

"Right. It belongs to the thee-ah-tuh," Charlie said with an overblown accent.

"We think." Peyton looked very solemn.

Lily shook her head slightly, feeling the dangly rhinestones brush against her neck. Then she gave the leather suitcase a final search. Tucked in a compartment in the bottom, she found a slightly weathered Playbill. She held her breath and examined the cover. The picture showed Dorothy, The Tin Man, The Scarecrow, and The Cowardly Lion. A yellow brick road stretched out beneath them.

"*The Wizard of Oz!*" she exclaimed, her eyes widening. Her friends crowded around to look at the theater booklet. Its pages were yellowed, but the Playbill was otherwise in pristine condition. Lily opened it, being careful not to tear the brittle paper. "What a coincidence! And look. It's signed by the cast," she said breathlessly.

Lily ran her fingers over their names, imagining what it would be like to be a Broadway star. Then she flipped through the final pages. Elise leaned in, squinting.

"I wonder what that's all about." She pointed at a blank spot on the page, and her friends looked closer.

"What?" Charlie asked.

"There's nothing there," Lily added.

Elise peered over the top of her glasses, her eyes widening. She slipped the glasses on and off, leaning in even farther, her dark ponytail brushing the page.

Peyton eyed her quizzically. "What—are those glasses making you see things?" she asked jokingly.

"Yes!" Elise gasped. She slid the frames onto Lily's nose and put the page in front of her. Lily almost dropped the book.

Chapter 4

PEYTON TOOK the glasses and the Playbill, and read out loud:

Use what you find. Employ your powers for good causes, not evil deeds. Together you will solve many mysteries.

Good Luck!

"See the bold letters?" she asked. "They spell something: S-P-Y S-O-C-I-E-T-Y."

"Spy society," Elise echoed. "Is that a play?"

"I don't think so." Peyton shook her head. "I think this stuff might not be intended for the theater at all. I think it might be . . ."

"Spy gear," Charlie finished.

Elise laughed. "Spy gear? Isn't that a little far-fetched? All this stuff looks pretty normal to me."

"Doesn't sound far-fetched so much as crazy," Lily piped up. "I mean, what would *we* do with spy gear, anyway? We're not undercover agents; we're theater people."

"Speak for yourself," Charlie protested. "I'm not a spy or a drama geek. No offense."

Peyton clapped her hands to get everyone's attention. "Ladies," she said. "You read it yourself. We have to—"

Just then the door swung open, and Celia Durham appeared. Peyton frowned. Celia played Glinda the Good Witch and spent a *lot* of time being too good to be true. She loved to mention how great her costume was going to be and how beautiful she'd look in her poofy pink dress. Right now Celia was wearing a small smile that rubbed Peyton the wrong way. "Rehearsal is starting, ladies," she said in perfect imitation of the real director, Ms. Curtan.

Peyton felt a wave of guilt and looked at her watch. As

assistant director, it was *her* job to call rehearsals. She'd totally missed her cue! "Oh man!" she said, jumping up. "We have to go!"

Celia turned on her heel. "You're welcome," she said, though nobody had thanked her. "Oh, and I told Ms. Curtan we can't use that dog," she called over her shoulder. "They aren't allowed on school grounds!"

Peyton sighed. She hated being late, and had planned to talk to Ms. Curtan herself about having Bowzer play Toto. He'd be perfect! But Celia had beaten her to the punch . . . twice. "Ladies, we'll have to sort out this spy stuff later," Peyton said. "We've got to start rehearsal."

Charlie grabbed her dog to leave, but Peyton stopped her. "Bowzer should stay, no matter what Celia says. Ms. Curtan needs to see him in action."

Charlie patted Bowzer's head. "Okay, Toto," she told her pup. "You're on. But I don't think we're in Kansas anymore!" She slipped him into Dorothy's basket. "I'll be in the wings in case you need me to wrangle the beast," she said jokingly.

Lily nodded and followed Peyton onto the stage,

where kids had gathered for rehearsal. While Elise got to work taping a yellow brick road onto the floor, Peyton crossed to center stage with the Flash Magic tucked under her arm and her marked-up script in her hand.

Despite Celia's warning, Ms. Curtan didn't seem to have arrived yet, but Peyton thought she should go ahead and get her cast working. "All right, everyone, we're going to start at the beginning and get through as much blocking as we can." As assistant director, part of her job was to tell people where to stand in each scene. She flipped to the first page. "We're in Kansas, and Dorothy is out for a walk when the tornado hits. Dorothy?"

Lily stepped forward with a flourish, still wearing the necklace and earrings. Celia's mouth dropped open when she spotted the vintage bling. "Oh my gosh! That necklace is perfect! It would look divine with my Glinda costume!" She strode up to Lily, arms reaching for the jewels.

Lily's hand covered the necklace protectively, but before she could ward the good witch off, Celia grabbed ahold of it. Then Bowzer, who had been totally quiet until now, jumped out of the basket and started barking. For a little dog, he had a big bark.

Celia reeled, yanking the necklace and breaking the clasp. The necklace fell, rhinestones clattering on the wooden floor. Celia ran upstage like she was being chased by a tiger, and Bowzer played along by darting after her.

"Bowzer, no!" Charlie rushed out from the wings to wrangle her pup.

Lily dropped to her knees to pick up the broken choker.

"Stay focused, people," Peyton shouted uselessly into the din.

Scooping Bowzer into her arms, Charlie quieted him with a treat. He wagged his tail and looked at Celia, his tongue lolling. "He likes you," Charlie told Celia with a shrug.

Celia sniffed, then pouted at Lily like it was all her fault the choker was broken. "Never mind about that old thing," Celia eventually said. "My Glinda will have plenty of sparkle without it. Besides, everyone knows it's bad luck to wear real jewelry onstage. You can curse the whole show."

Lily's blue eyes were full of worry. Breaking the mysterious necklace seemed like bad luck enough.

"That's just silly superstition," Elise said firmly. She took the choker out of her friend's hands. "Don't worry. I can fix it," she said, so quietly only Lily and Peyton could hear.

Peyton saw Lily's eyebrows rise. Her hands reached up to her ears. "Say that again," Lily whispered to Elise.

"What, that I can fix this?" Elise asked, confused.

Lily nodded and leaned in to whisper something to Elise. Elise gaped at her friend, then nodded and hurried offstage.

What are they talking about? Peyton was dying of curiosity but stopped herself from rushing up to Lily. She was the assistant director, and the real director was still nowhere to be seen. It was her job to get the show back on the road.

"Back into your basket, Toto," Charlie said, plopping him into the wicker carrier.

"Let's get back to the scene. Dorothy?"

Dorothy stepped forward; then she and Toto strolled across the stage on their Kansas "walk."

"Good, good," Peyton said. "Try not to turn your back to the audience." She turned a page in her marked-up script and was about to give her next bit of blocking when an elderly man came up the stairs, stage right. Peyton held her hand up, a signal to hold the scene.

"Can I help you?" she asked, feeling a twinge of annoyance. Couldn't he see that they were working?

"No, no. I'm fine," He strolled slowly and casually across the stage, looking around and clucking his tongue.

Bowzer jumped out of the basket to sniff the newcomer's pant cuff.

"Um, excuse me, this is a rehearsal," Peyton tried again.

The man gave her a long look down his long nose, and adjusted his bow tie. "Is it?" he asked, looking up at the lights.

Peyton looked at Lily. *Who was this guy?*

"Yes. It is. And you are interrupting it. Could you

please leave the stage?" Peyton added. She could feel herself losing her patience.

The man didn't move for a moment. He gave her a stern look, then broke into a half smile. "Finally!" he said. "That took you far too long, young lady. If you are going to direct a show, you must learn to direct *anyone* who comes into your theater. You have to be in charge!"

Peyton swallowed hard. Wasn't that what she was trying to do?

"Walter Zade!" Ms. Curtan appeared from backstage, smiling. "How nice to see you!"

Mr. Zade extended a hand. "Sylvia," he greeted. "Nice to see you. I hope I'm not intruding—I simply had to come and see what everyone is talking about. Proctor's new theater is creating quite a buzz."

"Isn't it lovely?" Ms. Curtan remarked proudly. "Would you like one of our students to give you a tour?"

Mr. Zade shook his head. "Not necessary. I've seen quite enough." He wrinkled his nose. "Why we needed a new theater is beyond my comprehension. We put on countless wonderful productions in the old one. Glitter and gloss simply hide weak performances, don't you think?"

Peyton's jaw dropped as Charlie slipped Bowzer into the basket for a third time. Who was this Walter Zade guy?

Lily must have felt insulted, too. "We're excited about our new theater," she said, walking up to him boldly. "We're going to put on a great show,"

The old man's narrow eyes glinted. "I'd like to see that," he challenged. Then Mr. Zade noticed that he was standing over the new trapdoor, and quickly hopped off. "How do you know all these high-tech contraptions even work?" he asked.

The cast and crew stared at him, speechless. And with that, Walter Zade exited the stage as unexpectedly as he had arrived.

Chapter 5

ELISE FELT a tingle as she looked down at the rhinestone necklace on the workbench. She hoped she could repair the clasp, because this was not just any ordinary jewelry. The beautiful vintage piece was also a spy device! Picking it up, she examined it closely, trying to see where the microphones were located. She knew there had to be some, because Lily had just told her that the necklace was transmitting sounds to the earrings! They certainly were well hidden. . . .

Taking out a pair of pliers, Elise carefully re-created the O shape in the final link in the silver chain. Then she reattached the old-fashioned clasp. Her hands shook slightly, and it took three tries. Finally, the clasp was repaired.

She slipped the necklace around her neck to make sure it would hold and momentarily admired the glittering stones in the mirror. Then, leaving the necklace on the worktable, she went to check on Dorothy's house.

Dorothy's house was Elise's favorite set piece. She'd spent too much time building it, she knew, but was proud of the fact that it was made of reclaimed lumber and hardware. Even the door handles were real, old, and reused. On one side it was Dorothy's house in Kansas. On the other, it was the "dropped in Munchkinland" version, complete with The Wicked Witch of the East's "legs" sticking out at the bottom. The whole thing could spin, transforming for its "landing" in Oz.

Elise opened the door on the Kansas side and stepped in. Closing her eyes, she twirled in a circle to get the feeling of being in a tornado. She could hear Peyton giving instructions onstage, "No backs to the audience!" "Tell it to the people in the last row!" Elise smiled. Her friend was a born director!

Stopping before she got too dizzy, Elise threw open the Oz door and stepped out of the house. She was only backstage, but she could still feel the excitement of the moment. The production was going to be great!

"Welcome to Oz," said a voice.

Blinking in surprise, Elise opened her eyes to see Charlie standing there holding a magic wand and wearing the necklace she'd left on the bench, along with Glinda's sparkling tiara!

"Oh, thank you," Elise said with a smirk. "But who are you?"

"I am Glinda, the Good Witch of the North," Charlie replied in a girly voice. "I was in my magic transportation bubble when it burst and I landed backstage."

Elise giggled. "You are a drama girl at heart, Charlie Lopez," she pronounced.

"I was a little bored," Charlie confessed, shrugging. Just then Bowzer started barking onstage. "But there's my cue!" she added with a laugh. "I think my pup needs a little onstage guidance. And maybe a potty break!" Shedding the Glinda gear and shoving it at Elise, Charlie sprinted onto the stage.

Elise watched, shaking her head. After checking Dorothy's house one more time, she headed to the prop room. She had just finished organizing the Munchkin costumes when the space was flooded with people all talking at once. The whole cast was in an uproar! Elise stepped out of the prop room just in time to see Lily limp over to an empty chair.

"Are you sure you're all right?" Celia hovered over Lily. "You could have broken a leg . . . literally!"

Lily looked very pale. Behind them, Peyton was uncharacteristically silent.

Elise waited for Peyton to explain that Celia was overreacting. She waited for Lily to say it was no big deal. But both of them just gave her worried looks. This was not acting. This was bad.

"What happened?" Elise finally asked.

"The latch on the trapdoor failed, and the door fell open at the end of Dorothy and The Scarecrow's big number. Lily almost fell in," Peyton explained.

"She was inches from her doom!" Celia wailed.

"I'm fine," Lily insisted. But Elise caught the knowing look in her eyes. Lily clearly had more to tell her.

"*Everyone* is fine," Peyton added. "It was just a little alarming."

Elise nodded slightly and turned her attention to the work that still needed to get done. She would talk to Lily later. With the run-through over, the Munchkins were ready for their costume fittings. Black-and-white-striped stockings and green shirts were being yanked off the racks, and she needed to write down who was taking what.

"Easy, Munchkins," Elise called. "There's a costume for everyone."

Josh Erdly, the boy playing The Cowardly Lion, sat down heavily on a stool and pointed to the earrings Lily still wore. "This proves it. The show is cursed," he announced. "It's that jewelry."

"What if it's not just superstition?" one of the winged monkeys asked.

"I read about a production being cursed," said Ethan, The Scarecrow. "The lead ended up in the hospital!"

"What if that happens to one of us?" one of the Munchkins whimpered. She was holding a green shirt up to her torso for sizing.

"That looks perfect," Elise said, moving on to the next Munchkin.

"It won't happen to any of us," Peyton said firmly. "The show is not cursed. We just had a rough rehearsal. That's all."

Elise sighed. A bad rehearsal was never good for morale, and despite Peyton's attempts to calm everyone, she could tell people were still unsettled. And so was she.

The trapdoor had been working perfectly—Elise had checked it herself that morning before school. She'd even admired the sturdy magnetic latch, noting that it had to be intentionally set to open; its default setting was locked. "I'll be back in a sec," she told her friends.

Elise walked onto the empty stage. Kneeling down, she peered at the latch. She was wondering if it had been tampered with when a message floated in front of her eyes.

"Huh?" She put her hands to her face. She'd forgotten that she was wearing the prop glasses! And the lenses were obviously more than plain glass—they were a heads-up display! Words had appeared on the insides of her lenses, like a computer screen. Someone, somewhere, was sending her a message! She took the glasses off and looked at the front. The message was invisible. She put them back on and read:

We're off to see the wizard.

What was that supposed to mean? And who the heck was sending the message?

Chapter 6

"YOU DID great in there, Bowze," Charlie said as they strolled across Proctor Middle's field. "Especially chasing Celia. But we're going to have to work on your stage presence. You need to bark at The Wicked Witch of the West like you really mean it!" She couldn't help but give her dog a few pointers—she'd been listening to Peyton direct for years! Still, Charlie was amazed by Bowzer's calm demeanor. Watching rehearsal had made *her* antsy enough to play dress-up!

While Bowzer stopped to sniff a fresh patch of grass, Charlie stuck a hand in her pocket and touched something smooth and hard. A second later she pulled out the pocket watch from the suitcase. She'd forgotten all about it! Pushing a little button on the side of the case, she slid the watch out. She'd been reluctant to crack open the suitcase but had to admit the stuff inside was pretty cool. Still, it was hardly James Bond gear. How could some old watch help a person spy and "solve many mysteries," like the secret writing had said? She was about to slide the watch back into its case when she noticed a tiny toothpicklike thingy inserted into the inside.

"What is that for?" she wondered aloud, unclipping it. It was cool, smooth, and tiny, and one end had a rounded point like a pencil. She was rolling the small stick back and forth between her fingers when the watch slipped out of her palm. She snatched it up almost as soon as it hit the grass, panicked that she'd broken it. To her surprise, the winder clicked and the face slid slightly off the base.

Oh no! It's ruined! But then she saw it was actually *supposed* to slide. She pushed the face up and around, revealing a tiny keyboard underneath.

"Whoa," Charlie murmured. She hadn't been buying the whole spy mission theory. . . . It sounded more like a television drama than the wonderful land of Oz. But this was *not* an ordinary pocket watch!

Excited to try out the tiny keyboard, Charlie used the stylus to type on the teeny keys. She tapped the first thing that came into her head, groaning to herself at the same time. It was a song from the play! For a girl who wasn't into theater, she knew waaay too much about this show. It was like the soundtrack to *The Wizard of Oz* was playing in her brain *all the time*! Charlie was shaking her head to get the music out when she realized that the music she was hearing wasn't in her head at all—it was coming from behind the bleachers a few yards away.

Looking closer, she spotted Teresa Gordon and her friend Shawna Hayes—the school's top two violinists—playing. The annoying duo was practicing *Wizard of Oz* songs!

All at once Charlie was suspicious, because the orchestra wasn't going to accompany the show like it usually did, and she knew from Teresa that its members were grouchy about it. Their conductor was on leave, and had decided to wait until spring and do an orchestra-only show. So why were Teresa and Shawna practicing that particular music? It seemed totally fishy.

The girls finished playing, and Charlie slid the watch back into its case before creeping closer. The bleachers provided good cover.

"I can't believe we have to wait until spring to perform," Teresa complained.

"Don't worry," Shawna replied. "We'll get our moment in the limelight . . . and maybe sooner than you think."

"Really?" Teresa whined.

Charlie heard another whine . . . Bowzer whimpering at her feet.

"Shhhhh," she warned him. Tugging gently on his leash, she turned back toward the theater before they could be seen.

Lost in thought, Charlie was pulling Bowzer along when she saw Elise, Lily, and Peyton coming her way. Lily was still in her gingham Dorothy dress. Peyton had the suitcase. They were walking toward her, fast!

"We have to powwow at my house," Peyton explained, lifting the case and thumping it with the palm of her free hand. "There's more to this stuff than meets the eye."

"I'll say," Charlie agreed, falling into step with her friends. She couldn't wait to show them the watch. Maybe they could figure out why it had a keypad. . . .

Seven minutes later the girls were piled into Peyton's tiny bedroom with the Spy Society stuff spread on the bed.

Lily explained how the earrings and the necklace worked together. "The necklace is a transmitter, and the earrings are receivers," she said. "With the earrings on, I could hear everything that happened around the necklace."

Charlie looked a little sheepish. "Everything?"

Lily nodded. "Yes, *Glinda*. So sorry to hear about your bubble!"

"Busted!" Elise chortled. The girls all laughed, and then Lily grew serious. "I also overheard something when you were walking Bowzer."

Charlie's hands went up to the necklace. She'd forgotten she was still wearing it! When she listened in on Shawna and Teresa's conversation, it transmitted right to Lily's ears!

"Shawna sounded pretty sneaky when she said they'd get their moment in the limelight sooner rather than later," Lily said worriedly.

"That's exactly what I was thinking," Charlie agreed.

"The plot thickens," Peyton said mysteriously. "I just wish I knew what secret use the Flash Magic has."

"I'm still not clear on these glasses, either," Elise said. "They're definitely not just prop glasses, though. I mean, they read that message in the Playbill. And they've got a HUD."

"A what?" Lily asked.

"A heads-up display. The inside of the glasses is kind of like a computer screen, and words appear on it. But I can't quite figure out where they're coming from. . . ."

"Words? Like messages?" Peyton asked.

"Sort of. So far I've gotten: *We're off to see the wizard.*"

"Strange," Peyton murmured.

"Not so strange," Charlie countered. She picked the watch up off the bed and showed her friends the miniature keyboard and stylus hidden inside. "That's what I typed on here, only I had no idea where I was sending it!"

Peyton was thoughtful. "Okay, so the Flash Magic is a mystery, but the watch can send messages to the glasses, and the necklace picks up sound for the earrings."

"This *is* some serious spy stuff," Charlie confirmed.

"Right. And we're supposed to use it for good," Lily said, remembering the message.

"What the heck do you think that means?" Charlie asked. She typed, *Who are we supposed to spy on?* on the tiny keyboard.

Elise read the screen on her glasses. "Oh, I forgot to tell you," she said. "Somebody definitely messed with the trapdoor. There's no way it could have come unlocked by itself. I think we should use our new spy gear to figure out who doesn't want this show to go on."

Chapter 7

"WELL, *I* don't think they should break school rules for anyone . . . or any*thing*," Celia complained into the makeup mirror. Lily bit her lip and tried not to roll her eyes. Celia was bent out of shape because Ms. Curtan had agreed to let Bowzer play Toto in spite of the "no dogs on school grounds" rule.

"I don't know what you're so worried about," Lily said. "It's not like you're allergic. And you don't have to carry him around—I do." She scratched the terrier under the chin.

Celia squished her lips together and squinted at the dog, who was getting settled in Dorothy's basket. "I'm only concerned for the good of the show."

"I know," Lily said, even though she didn't. Celia was probably just afraid of being upstaged by a dog. After all, Bowzer was irresistibly cute. "But casting Bowzer *is* for the good of the show. He's way more realistic than a stuffed toy."

Celia nodded and both girls studied their reflections in the giant makeup mirror. Lily knew Charlie suspected the orchestra girls were trying to mess up the show, but Celia's constant complaining was suspicious, too. Could she be behind some of the "accidents"?

Lily shook the thought from her mind. Celia was *seriously* into being onstage. She wouldn't do anything to jeopardize her time in the spotlight.

The two girls fiddled with their makeup and hair, trying to perfect their characters' looks. Dorothy's makeup was okay—as a farm girl she just needed enough blush and eyeliner to help her features stand out from a distance. The hair, though, was a problem. Since Lily was blonde, she needed a wig. Only, the brown braided wig she had was hideous. It poufed out at the back and sides, making her look like she had two ropes hanging off her head. Plus it was hot and itchy. The only *good* thing about it was that it hid the spy earring she wore.

Lily tugged the wig down and caught a glimpse of the rhinestones on her left lobe. Peyton was wearing the other earring on her right ear, which meant *both* of them could hear whatever was going on near Elise. It was pretty cool that the three of them were connected from all different parts of the theater. Lily just wished she could talk into the earring, too, so her friends could hear *her*.

Lily readjusted the wig to hide her sparkle, even though Celia was too busy applying glitter to her eyelids to notice anything. The last thing she needed was to get everyone talking about the stupid curse again.

"Maybe you should dye your hair," Celia suggested, eyeing the ugly wig. "I'm going to dye mine platinum blonde! Won't that be perfect?"

Lily had to look away from her reflection. Dyed hair *would* look way better than the wig. "I wish," Lily said with a sigh. "But there's no way my mom would let me." She bit back a twinge of jealousy and dabbed a little more color on her lips.

"Really? Not even brown?" Celia asked, incredulous.

"Really," Lily sighed. Her mom was a stickler when it came to piercings, dyes, and makeup (other than stage makeup).

"You should ask," Celia encouraged.

Lily stuck her tongue out at the wig. It looked like some sort of two-tailed animal was making a home on her head. She picked up her phone. Celia was right, for once. She *should* ask.

Lily pressed "send" on her text message just as the light in the green room began to blink. It was time to go on. As she prepared to take the stage she heard mumblings in her left ear. She tapped the back clasp of the earring to turn up the volume and listened.

Elise must have left the necklace on her workbench, because the voice Lily heard was not her friend's. There were two voices, Jonah Kazinski and Ryan Seng. The Munchkins must have been holding the necklace, because it sounded like they were yelling in her ear.

"What, are you scared?" Jonah asked.

"No!" Ryan protested. "Just a little superstitious. Maybe we should throw this thing away."

Lily gasped. He had to be talking about the necklace! She was wondering what to do when Peyton's voice rang over the PA system.

"All Munchkins to the stage immediately," she said. Lily smiled to herself. Not only was Peyton listening; she was taking action!

Double-checking to make sure her earring was still hidden, Lily stepped onto the stage and into total chaos. Walter Zade was talking to Ms. Curtan. She had informed the cast that Walter would be "helping" with the rehearsals from now on, much to their dismay. Munchkins were everywhere. And Peyton looked very s-t-r-e-s-s-e-d.

Lily felt for her friend. Peyton was working hard to make the show a success. But between Walter's ideas about how everything should be done and Ms. Curtan's distractedness, the assistant director job was now extra challenging. Peyton was literally running the show.

"Come on, people!" Peyton shouted, clapping her hands to coax the hesitant Munchkins into position. Nobody wanted to be near the trapdoor, which created odd gaps onstage.

Lily crossed to the adults. Maybe she could help out by getting Walter offstage.

"I never trust new construction," Walter was saying. "The wood is too green to be sturdy!" He pounded on the farmhouse for effect.

"Woof!" Bowzer protested.

"Here's Toto," Charlie said, handing the pup—and his basket—to Lily.

Lily scowled at Walter. She agreed with Bowzer! Everything Elise built was totally sturdy! She had mounted the house on wheels so it could spin easily. *And* it was two houses in one! Lily could hardly wait to climb into it in Kansas and emerge in the land of Oz.

"This monstrosity is overbuilt." Walter slapped the house's side once more. "We're illusionists, not architects!"

Lily frowned. Yes, Elise had probably spent too much

time on the set piece. But if Walter wanted to inspire them to greatness (the reason he claimed he was hanging around), he ought to stop putting them down! Lily had half a mind to tell Walter exactly that. She planted her fists on her hips and pointed her ruby slippers in his direction. But before she could open her mouth, Celia appeared in front of her.

"Guess what? My mom just went to Discount Beauty and got my hair dye. I'll be perfectly Glinda!" She held a box of Pure Platinum up to her head. "And she donated this for the people of Oz!" She grabbed Peyton by the arm and dragged her over to some boxes of semipermanent green dye.

Lily's heart sank. If everyone else had real hair, her wig look would look even weirder!

Celia spun around, still crooning about her soon-to-be-golden locks. "Oh, and, Lily," she said, nearly bumping into her. "I asked her to get you plain mousy brown. . . . Just in case your mommy will let you use it."

Lily stared longingly at the box. Over her shoulder she heard somebody snort. "Humph," Mr. Zade puffed again before registering his next complaint. "Wigs were good enough when I was running things," he grumbled.

Lily felt as though she'd been smacked.

Chapter 8

PEYTON WAS losing control . . . again! It seemed like every rehearsal started out okay, then steered itself right off the rails. And it usually happened right when Walter Zade started in with his not-so-helpful comments. Of course there were a few million other things going on, too. Like Glinda pretending to do a waltz with her box of hair dye.

"Glinda, you're going to look great. But I need you to do your magical dance backstage until it's your cue," she said as patiently as she could.

While Celia twirled off, Peyton put two fingers in her mouth and did her best taxi whistle. It was loud, and a second later the entire theater was quiet. Finally!

"Places, people! Act one, scene one . . . take one million," she added to herself in a whisper.

The cast and crew took their places, but Peyton sensed their reluctance. Rumors about the curse still hadn't died. And Peyton knew she wasn't doing any good by suspecting the cast and crew. Not that she and her friends had a choice. They had to find out who was behind the mishaps!

Suspects appeared in her mind's eye as she watched Dorothy sing "Over the Rainbow." Lily's voice was strong and right on pitch, but she looked a little tired. And Peyton needed to talk to Elise about her wig. It was starting to look like a regurgitated fur ball.

"All's quiet on the southern front." Elise's voice crackled in Peyton's ear. Peyton had almost forgotten about the receiver earring tucked under her newsboy cap! Elise was stationed beneath the stage, keeping an eye on the trapdoor. The girls were using the gear in a kind of spy assembly line. Lily and Peyton could hear Elise. Elise could get messages on her glasses from

Charlie. Charlie was now stationed outside the theater, watching for anything suspicious.

"Charlie says nothing to report," Elise relayed.

"Good," Peyton muttered. Maybe the cast would get through the whole show tonight. They desperately needed to, because opening night was less than a week away!

It was time for the twister, and they needed a couple more hands to turn the house. Once they had four people pushing, the house spun beautifully. It "landed" in Oz just as the other set pieces were placed and the hay blanket pulled back to reveal the yellow brick road. It all worked perfectly!

Peyton clasped her hands together and waited for Lily to make her entrance. It was Peyton's favorite scene in the movie, the moment when the film turns to color. She held her breath and waited. And waited. "Cue Dorothy," she called.

Nothing, and then . . .

"Help!" Lily's voice called plaintively.

Peyton saw that the house was rattling. Dorothy

hadn't missed her cue. She couldn't get out!

"Can somebody help her with the door?" Peyton called. A few Munchkins started pulling the door handle. "Try the back," Peyton shouted. But no matter how many people pulled, the doors stayed shut.

"Both doors are stuck!" The Cowardly Lion reported. "She's trapped!"

Through her earring Peyton could hear Elise fuming as she climbed out from under the stage to inspect the problem. "Somebody filled the locks with some kind of glue!" she informed Peyton. "Hang on, Lil. I'm going to have to take the hinges off."

Peyton let her head drop. So much for getting through the whole show! She looked around for Ms. Curtan, who seemed to have disappeared.

"That's a wrap," she told everyone miserably.

• • •

An hour later the four friends were sitting together, dangling their legs over the edge of the stage. Peyton looked down the row. Lily pulled at a lock of hair and stared at her phone. Elise gazed forlornly at a glue-filled door handle and door plate—her ruined masterpiece. And Charlie stroked Bowzer's soft fur and mumbled to herself, probably wondering how she'd gotten involved in this disaster.

It will be a miracle if we can pull off this show, Peyton thought with a sigh. *And an even bigger miracle if we can get to the bottom of the stage curse.*

Luckily Peyton was a big believer in long shots. And she knew she was like the captain of a ship. She needed to inspire her crew. Pronto.

Peyton hopped off the stage, turned her cap to a dashing angle, and began pacing in front of her friends. "Okay," she said, clapping her hands to signal that it was time to stop moping. "Somebody is definitely messing with our show. Curses don't know how to operate glue guns."

Charlie scowled. "I bet it's the orchestra girls," she said. "We all heard them the other day."

Elise looked thoughtful. "Maybe," she said. "But I don't think they're the only ones who want us off the stage."

"Yeah, Celia has been complaining . . . about everything," Lily offered.

Elise nodded. "True. And has anyone else noticed that right after Walter grouches about something, it seems to fall apart?"

Peyton smiled grimly. Apparently she was not the only one who saw suspects everywhere she turned! "You're all right," she said. "So we have at least three suspects."

"I don't think Celia would do anything to jeopardize her time onstage," Elise said.

Peyton nodded. "Good point. I'd say that either the orchestra girls or the old guy could be cast as our villains. But we need to have some callbacks before we can assign the role."

"Can you repeat that in English?" Charlie's brow was scrunched in confusion.

"We need to keep an eye on Walter and the orchestra girls, and find out which of them is sabotaging us."

"It's going to be tricky," Elise said slowly. "Because we have to keep working on the show."

"Do we ever," Peyton agreed. "But I definitely think we can do it."

Lily's phone beeped, signaling that she had a message. "My mom will be here in five minutes," she said, reading. "And—she's going to let me dye my hair!"

"Excellent," Peyton said as the girls gathered up their things. "That wig was—"

"Horrible!" Lily exclaimed with a grimace. She pushed open the theater door and they stepped into the night.

Outside it was dark, and they walked to the curb to wait for Lily's mom. "Can I see the flashlight?" Lily asked. "I need to see what color I'm going to be!"

Peyton handed over the light and Lily shined it on the box of dye Celia had left for her "in case." "Nutmeg!" Lily practically shrieked. "Doesn't that sound glamorous?"

Peyton felt a sharp tug on her sleeve.

"Look!" Charlie whispered. She motioned with her head toward the patch of grass between the school and the theater. It took a second for Peyton's eyes to adjust after gazing into the light of the flashlight, but when they did she saw what Charlie wanted them to see. It looked like three figures moving across the lawn toward the theater—figures carrying violin cases. Peyton squinted into the distance. But it was too dark to make out any details, and a moment later Lily's mom was honking at the curb. Further investigation would have to wait.

Chapter 9

"CAN YOU place these onstage?" Elise asked, handing Walter some cornstalk stands. "The numbers on the stand correspond to the duct tape mark—"

Walter waved a dismissive hand. "Child, you do not need to direct *me*." He took a cornstalk, shuffling away and muttering something about no small parts, only small players.

Elise smiled. It had been a really good idea to keep Walter out of trouble by giving him things to do for the production. Her own to-do list was a mile long, so it felt good to cross off a few items and keep an eye on Walter at the same time. Turning away, she circled Dorothy's house and tested the new door handles. Both opened. She could cross that off, too.

She was heading backstage to find some finishing touches for the house when she glanced into the orchestra pit and saw a small cache of instrument cases.

That's weird, she thought. Why would there be violins down there? 1) They were using a CD soundtrack for the show, and 2) Nobody other than *Wizard* cast and crew was supposed to be practicing in the theater. Clearly, some orchestra members were breaking that rule. In her mind's eye, Elise saw the cluster of people prowling across the lawn outside the theater.

Elise was about to whisper her findings into her necklace when she turned and saw Peyton standing right behind her. *And* she was with a bunch of orchestra players . . . including Teresa and Shawna! Elise bit her tongue.

"Elise, these are our talented new winged monkeys," Peyton said. She sounded suspiciously upbeat, and Elise instantly understood. Just as she'd given Walter a job so she could keep him busy, Peyton had cast the girls in the show to keep them close. Smart!

The musicians looked a little nervous at the idea of performing *on* and not *next to* the stage. But Elise nodded, smiled, and welcomed them to the team. "Okay, let's find you guys some costumes," she said.

She led the reluctant actors to a rack of dark coats with tails sewn onto them. "Try this," she said, holding one up to Teresa.

And by the way, is that your violin case in the pit? she added to herself. But her thoughts were interrupted by a loud wail coming from the stage. Everyone hurried out to see what was going on.

"It's horrible!" Celia wailed. "Hoorrrible! Somebody switched the bottles, and I look like The Wicked Witch of the West!" With a melodramatic flourish, Celia pulled her hood off her head.

A collective gasp went up. Glinda's newly dyed hair was not a pretty platinum blonde. It was bright green!

Teresa and Shawna gathered around, clucking sympathetically. "My mom says I can't dye it again because it would be bad for my hair," Celia sobbed.

"What'd I say? Wigs work just fine," Walter muttered as he fiddled with the giant rainbow. It was on a rack system and slid on and off the stage.

Elise scowled at the old guy, suddenly wishing he wouldn't touch anything. "I think we can rule out Celia for good now," she whispered into her necklace. "She'd never dye her hair green on purpose!"

Elise saw Peyton nod slightly and look over at Celia. Then she cocked her hat and reminded everyone what they were there for. "Time for a run-through," she called loudly.

Celia was hastily shuffled offstage and everyone took their places. Everyone but Lily.

"Where's Dorothy?" Peyton called.

"Haven't seen her, come to think of it," Elise whispered into the necklace.

"Right here," Lily replied, appearing out of nowhere. She looked down as she walked and had a scarf over her hair.

"Uh-oh," Elise murmured.

"We're not doing *Fiddler on the Roof*," Peyton teased.

Lily's eyes began to water and Elise was flooded with worry for her friend. "I wish we were," Lily said, forcing a smile. Then she pulled off the bandanna and dropped her head into her hands. "Isn't it awful?" she said to the floor.

Peyton gasped. Elise's heart flew into her throat. Lily's hair was Marilyn Monroe blonde!

"This isn't the color on the box," Lily whimpered. "My mom is going to kill me!"

Elise rushed up to Lily. "It could be worse. Celia's hair is green." But she could hear the rumblings of the cast and crew. Two bad dye jobs. Two glued locks. The trapdoor. "You won't be the only one in a wig," Elise added, trying to sound cheerful despite Walter's voice in her head.

Elise rounded up Celia and Lily and herded the distraught girls to the makeup room. "The show must go on," she chirped as she shoved two newly acquired wigs on their heads. She had managed to find some better hairpieces, but they still looked pretty fake.

Lily handed Elise her spy earring as they headed back

to the stage. "I don't even want this right now," she confessed quietly. "You take it."

Elise squeezed her friend's arm. "Okay, but then you should wear this." She quickly put the necklace around Lily's neck, hiding it in the collar of her blouse.

"That was fast," Peyton told Elise when the girls reappeared. "And they look great. Now that that's done, can you help me find Toto?" Elise recognized the look in Peyton's eyes—worry. Charlie and Bowzer were missing. She wished her glasses could *send* messages and not just receive them. Why hadn't Charlie sent any news? She was supposed to arrive with Bowzer ages ago.

"We'll have to start without him," Peyton announced as Elise hurried away.

While she searched the school for signs of Charlie, Elise listened in on rehearsal and could tell it was going terribly! Dorothy tripped over a bale of hay. Glinda nearly crashed into the prop house. When Scarecrow bruised his shin on a signpost, Elise decided enough was enough and hurried back to the theater.

From the back of the house it was easy to see the

problem. All the set pieces were slightly misplaced. *Walter!* Elise thought in frustration. She squinted at the empty theater seats. "Has anyone seen Mr. Zade?"

Chapter 10

CHARLIE WAS on her way into the theater when she saw Walter coming out. The old man had his head down and was moving with determination. He looked like he had somewhere to be.

This would be a perfect opportunity for Charlie to follow Walter, put her spy skills to the test, and see if she could learn anything. For a split second she felt torn. She had Bowzer with her on a leash and the pup needed to get inside for rehearsal. But by the time she delivered him and got back outside, Walter would be gone!

Charlie thought Teresa and Shawna were trying to mess up the production. But Walter was a suspect, too, and Charlie was the only Spy Society member in sight. She had to stay with the suspect.

Luckily, the meddling guy traveled on foot. And he wasn't exactly fast. Charlie and Bowzer followed him easily at a distance, ducking behind trash cans and benches to stay out of sight. They were almost to the center of town when Charlie remembered the watch.

She pulled it out of her pocket to send a message to Elise while Bowzer pulled her along. For a small dog, Bowzer had a big tug. She typed as best she could and hit "send" as she rounded a corner. Stopping short, she pulled Bowzer back sharply. Walter was right there!

"Sorry, boy!" she whispered. "But we can't be seen!" She dropped to her knees and peeked around a giant bush.

Walter was standing outside the Prime Time Senior Center. He paused and took off his sunglasses, then pulled open the door.

Should she follow him inside? Charlie wasn't sure. But since he'd arrived at his destination, she could take a minute to write another message to Elise. *Zade is in Prime*

Time, she wrote. *Going to try to see.*

She slipped the stylus back into the side of the watch and walked around the senior center, a single-story building with lots of windows. Trees and shrubs surrounded it. She prowled, letting Bowzer lead and keeping her head lower than the bushes as she peeked into windows, looking for Walter. Finally she spotted him playing cards with a group of white-haired gentlemen.

Suspect in view, she typed. Except that when she looked back up, the suspect looked nothing like the suspect! Grumpy Walter Zade was smiling and laughing . . . and cracking up the other men at the table!

Charlie tried to wedge herself between the building and a woody shrub. No luck. She stepped onto a limb to get a better view. It still wasn't great. She took one more step up and *SNAP!*

The bush gave, and Charlie dropped the leash and fell to the ground, landing hard. Bowzer started barking like crazy.

"Shhh!" Charlie hissed. She reached for his snout to muzzle him, but he dodged. "This isn't a game, Bowzer.

Come!" But Bowzer dodged his master until she was totally out of breath.

"Fine, you win," she said, collapsing on the grass to catch her breath. Bowzer walked right up and licked her nose.

"Well, this looks like serious spy work." Elise's face in the cat-eye glasses appeared above Charlie's. She was grinning.

"Elise!" Charlie gasped. "Am I glad to see you!"

"Yeah, I thought you were watching TV, but I finally figured out your messages. You need spell-check!" She laughed. "So, did you lose him?"

"I think he's still inside," Charlie said, securing her dog to a tree. She tossed Bowzer a treat. "We must continue our surveillance!" she said in a secretive tone. She was loving this spy business!

Elise nodded, and Charlie led her back to the window where she'd last seen Walter. Elise peered through the glass, and her eyes widened in surprise.

"That's Walter?"

"I know, right?" Charlie agreed, peering in and gaping.

Walter was no longer playing cards—he was dancing a soft shoe!

Charlie and Elise watched, mesmerized. Then Walter missed a step, caught himself, and started laughing so hard he had to sit down. The whole senior center crowd was laughing along with him when Bowzer started barking again.

"I'll get him. You stay put." Elise slipped away as Charlie noticed for the first time that the window was unlatched. She opened it just a bit and leaned closer to hear the conversation inside. The seniors were getting back to their card game.

"How's your little theater plot coming along?" a man with a tweed hat asked.

"Have you infiltrated as you'd hoped?" asked a gentleman with a polka-dot bow tie.

"Of course!" Walter said with a chuckle. "The new theater troupe isn't going to know what's hit them. . . ."

Charlie blinked twice and nearly fell over backward. *Plot. Infiltrated. Hit.* Apparently the new Walter was still the old Walter, and more than just a suspect!

It's Walter! she tapped frantically into the watch. *Walter is the culprit!* She hurriedly replaced the stylus and looked back through the window for a final look at the perpetrator. But the card table was empty!

Chapter 11

OVER NEXT to Bowzer's tree, Elise took off her glasses and squinted at the message on the lens. It didn't make any sense. "'Alter is the pulpit'?"

Bowzer gave her a look that said he was more interested in dog treats than spy messages. Then he started to wiggle and bark.

"Shhh," Elise scolded. "We're on a secret—"

"We've got to tell the others!" Charlie shouted, sprinting up to them. She paused barely long enough to grab Bowzer's leash off the tree, then took off.

Tell the others . . . what? Elise wondered as she struggled to keep up. Charlie's wind sprints at basketball practice made her seriously fast. She ran the entire way back to school, too. By the time they saw the theater, Elise's lungs felt like they were going to burst.

The trio raced into the prop shop, where Peyton and Lily were bent over the Flash Magic. A thin red laser projected out of the long metal tube, and first aid stuff— from bandaging the bruised cast—was scattered on the table and floor.

"It's Walter!" Charlie blurted while Elise struggled to catch her breath.

"It's a trip wire!" Peyton replied, passing her hand through the thin red beam.

At that moment Elise finally figured out the message Charlie had sent to the glasses. "Oh!" she gasped. *"'Walter is the culprit'!"*

The revelations were flying, and Peyton and Lily looked stunned. Peyton tapped her index finger against her chin. "How do we know for sure?"

Charlie took a deep breath. "I heard him tell his friends that he was trying to infiltrate the theater!"

"Admission of guilt is good," Peyton said. "But it's

not proof."

Charlie squinted at Lily. "What happened to your hair?"

Lily reached a hand up to her ridiculously blonde tresses. "Ugh. Don't remind me," she groaned. She glanced at herself in the mirror, flinching. "My mom still hasn't seen it. Maybe I should wear those earrings, you know, to distract her." Elise and Peyton looked doubtful but tugged off their clip-ons and handed them over.

"It all makes sense," Elise said, bringing them back to the business at hand. "Walter has been upset about the new theater since the beginning. He's trying to shut us down. And now that we know it's him, we have to catch him in the act."

A slow smile spread across Peyton's face as she held up the flashlight. "And this little trip wire might be our ticket. We just need to set it up. Then we can catch anyone who sneaks into the theater to cause trouble!"

"Ooooooh," Elise said. "I know just where to set it." She led everyone over to the rainbow backstage. "Whatever Walter touches is the next thing that fails, right? Well, he was messing with *this* today. I didn't see anything wrong when I checked it over, but I bet he'll be back to screw it up."

Peyton pulled a section off the bottom of the Flash Magic and handed it to Charlie. "This piece is the receiver," she explained. "We need the beam of light to go right into it. Take it across the stage and find a spot that's sort of hidden."

Charlie carried it over and set it between the folds of the curtain. "It's in position," she called. Peyton aimed the beam of light across the stage, but aligning the two sides of the trip wire wasn't easy. Charlie got down on her hands and knees to try to capture the light. After a while Bowzer started to whine.

"I'll feed you in a sec," she said impatiently.

"I can feed him." Lily patted her leg, and Bowzer followed her into the wings.

Elise wanted to help with the trip-wire setup, but the space around the rainbow was tight, and Charlie and Peyton were on it. So she followed Lily to Bowzer's little feeding area.

While Lily filled the bowl, Elise peered out the window to the parking lot. The light outside was fading, but she could see two people talking by their cars. She did a double take. The two people were Ms. Curtan and Walter Zade!

Elise resisted the urge to race outside and drag Ms. Curtan away from the troublemaker. It wouldn't do any good, anyway. Crouching down beside Lily, she pointed out the window. "Walter is talking to Ms. Curtan!" she hissed.

Lily's eyes twinkled as she reached around to take off her necklace. "Let's do a little eavesdropping, shall we?" She reclasped the rhinestones on Bowzer, who had finished eating. Smiling mischievously, she opened the backstage door just enough for him to slip out.

Bowzer trotted over to the grass patch by the lot, moving closer to the adults. "He has a favorite tree out there," Lily said. "I hope it's close enough!" She handed Elise one of the earrings and they both grew silent as Bowzer moved into range.

"I can't believe I forgot my purse again," Ms. Curtan

was saying. "I can't keep track of anything!"

Lily and Elise exchanged looks. That explained why their *teacher* was here. . . .

Walter waved Ms. Curtan's worries away. "You have far too much to keep track of. That's why I'm glad I caught you, and why I'm sorry I can't be here to help with the remaining rehearsals."

Elise's eyebrows shot up. Did they just hear that?!

"I've got to go out of town to see my son. I'm on my way to the airport now," Walter went on. They chatted for a few more seconds, and then they hugged.

He's the bad guy! Elise wanted to shout.

"Woof!" Apparently Bowzer wanted to tell her, too.

"Here, Bowzer!" Elise slipped out the door and called the dog in a stage whisper. He came right away, and she snatched him up, but not before Walter turned and saw her. He squinted in the dim light, his face contorted into a scowl. Elise could practically hear him saying, "I'll get you, my pretty, and your little dog, too," as the door closed behind her.

Chapter 12

"SO LET me get this straight," Peyton said. "Walter is getting on a plane and won't be here for the rest of rehearsals?" She looked from Elise to Lily and back for confirmation. Then she broke into a huge smile. "That's the best news I've heard in an eon!"

"That's not all," Lily added. "We have a new spy in our society." She held up Bowzer, who looked undeniably dashing in the sparkly necklace. "His infiltration was top-notch." All four girls petted him at once. "Woof!" he said happily.

"The show actually has a chance of succeeding," Peyton murmured, half to herself and half to her friends.

She was sort of in shock.

"Why don't we go celebrate with milk shakes?" Charlie suggested. Peyton grinned. Charlie was always hungry! Come to think of it, Peyton was hungry, too. Her stomach had been in knots for so long she hadn't felt like eating. Right now she felt like she could eat everything on the Dairy Queen menu!

Apparently the other spies felt the same, because they all grabbed their bags and headed for the door. A minute later they were skipping up the sidewalk and singing, "We're off to see the Blizzard," with Charlie belting it out the loudest.

Gathered with the others around a table and sipping her shake, Peyton felt lighter than she had in ages. She'd actually begun to doubt the show was going to come together. "No more set pieces shifting, trapdoors opening, hair, well, dyeing." She looked at Lily apologetically. She hadn't meant to remind her.

"We have wigs for this." Lily sighed and held up a yellow lock of hair. "Think my mom will notice if I wear a wig at home?" The girls laughed.

Then, mid-sip, a really loud alarm went off. It sounded like a car alarm, only more intense. And it was coming from Charlie's pocket! Everyone in DQ turned to stare.

"What is that?" Peyton shouted over the blaring noise as she covered her ears. Charlie took the watch out of her pocket and the noise got even louder.

Bowzer, incognito in Charlie's backpack, began to bark like crazy. The Spy Society needed to get out of there, fast. The girls rushed outside while Charlie tried to muffle the noise. They hurried around the side of the DQ and into the alley.

"What's wrong with this thing?" Charlie asked, still trying to dampen the awful noise. "It's going haywire. I wish I'd never found that suitcase!" She gave up trying to quiet the noise and prepared to hurl the watch into the Dumpster.

All at once Peyton got the feeling the watch wasn't malfunctioning. She calmly took it from Charlie's hand and pushed a few buttons. The alarm stopped.

"Oh no," Elise said, looking a little cross-eyed in her

glasses. She was studying something on the HUD screen. "It says it's an alarm. Somebody set off the trip wire!"

Without another word the girls raced back to the theater. A million thoughts flew through Peyton's brain. *Walter is supposed to be gone. Did he come back? Or is someone else in there?*

Up ahead, Charlie was pulling open the door. Elise paused to look at the unlatched latch, and Peyton almost slammed into her.

"It's been taped over!" Elise announced as they took off again. The girls sprinted through the backstage rooms to the stage. Charlie slowed, and they tiptoed behind her toward the wings.

At least there are four of us, Peyton thought. *We can probably handle an old guy.*

But there was no old guy caught in the beam.

"Oh my gosh!" Peyton whispered as all four girls stared at what they'd caught.

Green-haired Celia was sashaying across the stage like she was the star of the show. Behind her, the rainbow had been painted over with giant black splotches.

"Dorothy's got to surrender now!" Celia cackled, sounding way more like a bad witch than a good witch. She gazed happily at a sparkling circle as though it were a crystal ball.

"What is that?" Charlie whispered.

Peyton turned pale. "It's the soundtrack!" she hissed. They had only one copy of it. It wasn't cheap, and had taken ages to get. If anything happened to it . . .

Peyton couldn't just stand there. "Hold it right there," she said, stepping out of the shadows.

Celia froze.

"I'll take that," Peyton said, reaching out a hand to take the disc.

Celia's expression went from surprised to frightened to friendly. Peyton thought maybe the girl was a better actress than she'd given her credit for, but she wasn't falling for it.

"What are you talking about?" Celia asked innocently, holding the disc behind her. "What are you doing here?"

"Celia, I know what you're up to," Peyton said evenly, looking from Celia to the still-damp, ruined rainbow.

"And so do we," Charlie added. She and the rest of the girls joined Peyton on the stage.

Celia's expression shifted again—only now she looked like a cornered emerald poodle. Her pent-up frustration and anger bubbled over.

"*I* was supposed to be Dorothy!" she hissed. "*I* was supposed to have all the lines, to get to sing. Glinda barely does *anything*!"

That's what this is all about? Peyton might have laughed out loud if it weren't so serious. And if Celia wasn't holding the disc. "So you were responsible for everything?" she asked.

Celia smiled like a cat with a canary in its jaws.

"But you could have really hurt Lily!" Charlie said accusingly.

"Yeah, and you ruined my house," Elise added.

"And my hair," Lily put in.

"Not to mention our show," Peyton said, taking a step closer. "Now hand over the disc."

Celia didn't bother denying anything. In fact, she looked rather proud of her villainousness . . . until Lily mentioned the hair.

"*Your* hair was supposed to be green!" Celia railed at Lily. "But Bowzer attacked me when I was switching the bottles around."

Peyton worked hard not to roll her eyes at the jealous girl. "Oh, come on, Celia. He wouldn't hurt a fly."

Celia stomped her foot in frustration.

"But what about Walter?" Charlie wondered.

"He made it so easy!" Celia gloated. "I just booby-trapped anything that old geezer mumbled about, and, voilà! The trapdoor was simple to rig in the open position and a little Internet research led me to fast-drying wood glue. But how do you like the rainbow . . . my newest creation?"

Peyton saw that Charlie was running out of patience. "You set him up, too?" she asked, incredulous. Frustrated, she lunged for the disc. The sudden move shook Bowzer loose from her pack, and he scrambled up over her shoulder and landed between Charlie and Celia. "Woof!"

With a high-pitched shriek, Celia turned, lost her

balance, and fell.

"Oh my gosh." Peyton heard a sharp crack in the din of the crash. And when Celia rolled over, her worst fear was realized. The soundtrack had broken into several pieces.

Celia kicked Bowzer away from her and glared at the four girls. "Ha!" she laughed defiantly. "You can't scare me."

"You won't get away with this," Charlie said menacingly. "Everyone will know you're responsible for ruining the show."

Celia laughed again. "Hmmm. Let's think. As far as anybody knows, the four of you were the last people here tonight, right? And you were supposed to check to make sure the door was locked behind you, right? Lucky for me, you left it open. Unlucky for you, I got in." Celia's tone was irritating, but that wasn't what was making Peyton's stomach clench. It was the fact that Celia was right. As assistant director, she was responsible for the door. She hadn't bothered to check it because it locked automatically. With Walter out of the picture, she'd thought she was in the clear!

"I'm going to claim I was never here. And you can't prove I was." Celia stood up and dusted herself off.

"But there are four of us to tell the truth," Lily pointed out.

Right before their eyes, Celia worked up some convincing mock tears. "But, Ms. Curtan, you know they're best friends. They're just jealous. That's why they're blaming me. That's why they did this to my hair. They want me out of the show!"

The four girls exchanged glances. Celia was a good actress.

"But the door was taped," Elise reminded everyone. "And if you didn't tape it . . ." She paused, looking at Celia.

"We did," a voice said from the orchestra pit. A bunch of tiny lights clicked on over music stands and the black space beside the stage lit up. The whole orchestra, including Teresa and Shawna, was there with their instruments out.

Peyton couldn't believe her eyes. What were they

doing there?

"We taped the door. We've been coming every night to practice," Teresa explained. "And we just heard everything."

On the stage, Celia melted into a puddle. The gig was up and she knew it. Taking on four girls with her acting skills was one thing; sticking to her lie against an orchestra pit full of eyewitnesses was another.

In the pit, Shawna played a few notes of "Ding-Dong! The Witch Is Dead." Onstage, the Spy Society shared high fives all around. Case closed!

Chapter 13

PEYTON TOOK a seat in the audience and tried to remain calm. It had seemed like this would never happen, like opening night would never come. But here it was! Peyton felt nervous for every single person involved in the play, including herself. But her job as assistant director was finished—the performance was in the talented hands of the cast and crew.

"Don't worry, sweetie," her mother said, giving her arm a squeeze. Peyton nodded but couldn't shake the thought that was spinning around and around in her head. *It will be a miracle if we pull this off!*

"Is this seat taken?" a familiar voice asked.

Peyton looked up and her heart skipped a beat. Walter Zade was back!

It's okay, she told herself. *He wasn't actually responsible for any of those mishaps! The production is safe!* Ms. Curtan had dealt with the real culprit harshly but fairly. Celia Durham had been assigned theater cleaning and would not be allowed to participate in any productions for a full year.

Peyton searched for a fingernail she hadn't already bitten down to the quick. When Walter leaned over a moment later, she held her breath. She really didn't need a crabby comment!

"Don't worry—it's going to be great," he whispered. "You've done a fantastic job."

Peyton squinted at him in the dim theater light. Was he being sarcastic?

Walter smiled warmly. "I knew you were director material from the minute I saw you."

Peyton was about to ask what he meant when the orchestra began to play. Her Flying Monkey herd was much thinner now, because the entire orchestra was in the pit, right where they belonged. Peyton just hoped they'd be able to stay awake! It was super lucky that Teresa and her friends had been sneaking into the theater to practice the songs. And they cheerfully stayed *very* late last night to get every note right.

Really, this whole show is a miracle, Peyton thought as Lily belted out her first song. This experience had been kind of like a twister that picked you up, twirled you around, and dropped you somewhere amazing—just like Dorothy on the stage.

At first Ms. Curtan had wanted to call the show off. But Peyton and her friends had argued that they couldn't let Celia defeat them. Of course, they couldn't let Celia be in the show after what she'd done, either. . . .

The stage filled with bubbles, the orchestra played tinkling music, and Glinda made a graceful entrance.

Peyton beamed, and Walter Zade chuckled. Who would have guessed that Charlie could be such a perfectly poufy princess?

"I am Glinda, the Good Witch of the North," she said clearly and sweetly. Luckily Charlie had spent so much time at rehearsals, she had picked up most of Glinda's lines. And they already knew the tiara would fit!

For the rest of the show Peyton let herself get lost. The sets were stunning. The music was awesome. Even Bowzer shone. Before Peyton knew it, the (freshly repainted) rainbow was being pushed onto the stage for the curtain call. The house erupted into applause. Walter stood up, leading the audience in a standing ovation.

Lily and Charlie beckoned Peyton to the stage, and Walter nudged her forward. Elise entered from the wings, and the girls took a bow. Peyton felt tingly all over.

As the curtain fell Peyton noticed a sophisticated-looking woman with dark glasses in the audience. By the time the lights came up she was disappearing through the door. Peyton stared after her. Had she just nodded knowingly in her direction?

"That was amazing!" Charlie cried as the curtain hit the floor.

Peyton turned her attention to her friends. "You were a fabulous Glinda." She patted Charlie on the back. All around them the cast and crew hugged and congratulated one another.

"We did it!" Teresa shouted, emerging from the pit with several musicians.

"It sounded great from down there!" Shawna added.

Peyton beamed at the players. "We couldn't have done it without you," she said.

Elise took out the old *Wizard of Oz* Playbill they'd found in the suitcase and showed it to Ms. Curtan as Walter appeared onstage.

"I couldn't have done this without you," Ms. Curtan told Walter and Peyton. "I've been so worried about finding a replacement for when I'm on maternity leave."

Peyton's eyes went wide. Maternity leave?

"But I found one," Ms. Curtan added, smiling at Walter.

"It will be my pleasure," Walter replied. Peyton was surprised to find that she was glad to hear that. The old guy was growing on her—and he really had "infiltrated" the theater group—but in a good way.

Walter peered at the Playbill and laughed. "Where'd you find this?" Peyton suddenly noticed a similarity between the smiling Scarecrow on the cover and Walter's grin.

"Is that you?" she asked, pointing. Walter's eyes gleamed as he nodded.

Peyton showed her friends the Playbill. "It's Walter!" she told them. Elise flipped through the pages, searching for more pictures of the young actor. A blank piece of paper fell out and fluttered to the ground. Elise picked it up, her eyes growing wide behind her glasses. She nudged Peyton and handed the glasses to her. Peyton donned them and looked at the page, which contained a brand-new spy message:

Congratulations. You did it, and without breaking a leg!
You used your key spy properties—ingenuity,
friendship, and confidence—to solve the mystery.
Your future is promising.

"G-O-O-D W-O-R-K! K-E-E-P I-T U-P," Peyton read as Charlie urged them out into the parking lot.

"I wonder who sent this? And who gave us all this stuff?" Elise mused.

"I don't even care," Charlie quipped. "Being a good

witch was exhilaratingly exhausting!"

A silver car idled in the parking lot. As the girls drew closer, the woman with the glasses pulled out. The girls stared after her until the silver car disappeared.

"Do you think she left us that suitcase?" Lily asked.

"Anything is possible," Peyton replied. Then she gave Lily one last note: "Click your heels, Dorothy. It's time to go home."

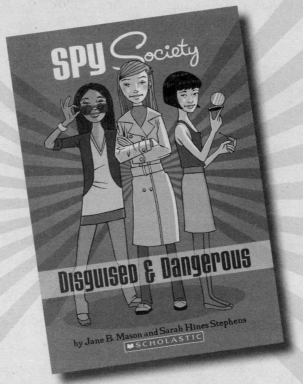